THE SLITHERING SHADOW
(XUTHAL OF THE DUSK)

BY

ROBERT E. HOWARD

British Library Cataloguing-in-Publication Data
A catalogue record for this book is available from the
British Library

Contents

Robert E. Howard. 1

Chapter I. 3

Chapter II 33

Chapter III 41

Chapter IV 49

Robert E. Howard

Robert Ervin Howard was born in Peaster, Texas in 1906. During his youth, his family moved between a variety of Texan boomtowns, and Howard – a bookish and somewhat introverted child – was steeped in the violent myths and legends of the Old South. Although he loved reading and learning, Howard developed a distinctly Texan, hardboiled outlook on the world. He became a passionate fan of boxing, taking it up at an amateur level, and from the age of nine began to write adventure tales of semi-historical bloodshed. In 1919, when Howard was thirteen, his family moved to the Central Texas hamlet of Cross Plains, where he would stay for the rest of his life.

At fifteen Howard began to read the pulp magazines of the day, and to write more seriously. The December 1922 issue of his high school newspaper featured two of his stories, 'Golden Hope Christmas' and 'West is West'. In 1924 he sold his first piece – a short caveman tale titled 'Spear and Fang' – for $16 to the not-yet-famous *Weird Tales* magazine. He published with the magazine regularly over the next few years. 1929 was a breakout year for Howard, in that the 23-year-old writer began to sell to other magazines, such as *Ghost Stories* and *Argosy*, both of whom had previously sent him hundreds of rejection slips. In 1930, he began a correspondence with weird fiction master H. P. Lovecraft which ran up to his death six years later, and is regarded as one of the great correspondence cycles in all of fantasy literature.

It was partly due to Lovecraft's encouragement that Howard created his most famous character, Conan the Cimmerian. Conan – a barbarian-turned-King during the Hyborian Age, a mythical period of some 12,000 years ago – featured in seventeen *Weird Tales* stories between 1933 and 1936, and is now regarded as having spawned the 'sword and sorcery' genre, making Howard's influence on fantasy literature comparable to that of J. R. R. Tolkien's. The Conan stories have since been adapted many times, most famously in the series of films starring Arnold Schwarzenegger.

Howard was enjoying an all-time high in sales by the beginning of 1936, but he was also deeply upset by the ill health of his mother, who had fallen into a coma. On the morning of June 11, 1936, he asked an attending nurse whether she would ever recover, and the nurse replied negatively. Howard walked to his car, parked outside the family home in Cross Plains, and shot himself. He died eight hours later, aged just thirty.

CHAPTER I

The desert shimmered in the heat waves. Conan the Cimmerian stared out over the aching desolation and involuntarily drew the back of his powerful hand over his blackened lips. He stood like a bronze image in the sand, apparently impervious to the murderous sun, though his only garment was a silk loin-cloth, girdled by a wide gold-buckled belt from which hung a saber and a broad-bladed poniard. On his clean-cut limbs were evidences of scarcely healed wounds.

At his feet rested a girl, one white arm clasping his knee, against which her blond head drooped. Her white skin contrasted with his hard bronzed limbs; her short silken tunic, lownecked and sleeveless, girdled at the waist, emphasized rather than concealed her lithe figure.

Conan shook his head, blinking. The sun's glare half blinded him. He lifted a small canteen from his belt and shook it, scowling at the faint splashing within.

The girl moved wearily, whimpering.

"Oh, Conan, we shall die here! I am so thirsty!"

The Cimmerian growled wordlessly, glaring truculently at the surrounding waste, with outthrust jaw, and blue eyes smoldering savagely from under his black tousled mane, as if the desert were a tangible enemy.

He stooped and put the canteen to the girl's lips.

"Drink till I tell you to stop, Natala," he commanded.

She drank with little panting gasps, and he did not check her. Only when the canteen was empty did she realize that he had deliberately allowed her to drink all their water supply, little enough that it was.

Tears sprang to her eyes. "Oh, Conan," she wailed, wringing her hands, "why did you let me drink it all? I did not know—now there is none for you!"

"Hush," he growled. "Don't waste your strength in weeping."

Straightening, he threw the canteen from him.

"Why did you do that?" she whispered.

He did not reply, standing motionless and immobile, his fingers closing slowly about the hilt of his saber. He was not looking at the girl; his fierce eyes seemed to plumb the mysterious purple hazes of the distance.

Endowed with all the barbarian's ferocious love of life and instinct to live, Conan the Cimmerian yet knew that he had reached the end of his trail. He had not come to the limits of his endurance, but he knew another day under the merciless sun in those waterless wastes would bring him down. As for the girl, she had suffered enough. Better a quick painless sword-stroke than the lingering agony that faced him. Her thirst was temporarily quenched; it was a false mercy to let her suffer until delirium and death brought relief. Slowly he slid the saber from its sheath.

He halted suddenly, stiffening. Far out on the desert to the south, something glimmered through the heat waves.

At first he thought it was a phantom, one of the mirages which had mocked and maddened him in that accursed desert. Shading his sun-dazzled eyes, he made out spires and minarets, and gleaming walls. He watched it grimly, waiting for it to fade and vanish. Natala had ceased to sob; she struggled to her knees and followed his gaze.

"Is it a city, Conan?" she whispered, too fearful to hope. "Or is it but a shadow?"

The Cimmerian did not reply for a space. He closed and opened his eyes several times; he looked away, then back. The city remained where he had first seen it.

"The devil knows," he grunted. "It's worth a try, though."

He thrust the saber back in its sheath. Stooping, he lifted Natala in his mighty arms as though she had been an infant. She resisted weakly.

"Don't waste your strength carrying me, Conan," she pleaded. "I can walk."

"The ground gets rockier here," he answered. "You would soon wear your sandals to shreds," glancing at her soft green footwear. "Besides, if we are to reach that city at all, we must do it quickly, and I can make better time this way."

The chance for life had lent fresh vigor and resilience to the Cimmerian's steely thews. He strode out across the sandy waste as if he had just begun the journey. A barbarian of barbarians, the vitality and endurance of the wild were his, granting him survival where civilized men would have perished.

He and the girl were, so far as he knew, the sole survivors of Prince Almuric's army, that mad motley horde which, following the defeated rebel prince of Koth, swept through the Lands of Shem like a devastating sandstorm and drenched the outlands of Stygia with blood. With a Stygian host on its heels, it had cut its way through the black kingdom of Kush, only to be annihilated on the edge of the southern desert. Conan likened it in his mind to a great torrent, dwindling gradually as it rushed southward, to run dry at last in the sands of the naked desert. The bones of its members—mercenaries, outcasts, broken men, outlaws—lay strewn from the Kothic uplands to the dunes of the wilderness.

From that final slaughter, when the Stygians and the Kushites closed in on the trapped remnants, Conan had cut his way clear and fled on a camel with the girl. Behind them the land swarmed with enemies; the only way open to them was the desert to the south. Into those menacing depths they had plunged.

The girl was Brythunian, whom Conan had found in the slave-market of a stormed Shemite city, and appropriated. She had had nothing to say in the matter, but her new position was so far superior to the lot of any Hyborian woman in a Shemitish seraglio, that she accepted it thankfully. So she had shared in the adventures of Almuric's damned horde.

For days they had fled into the desert, pursued so far by Stygian horsemen that when they shook off the pursuit, they dared not turn back. They pushed on, seeking water, until the camel died. Then they went on foot. For the past few days their suffering had been intense. Conan had shielded Natala all he could, and the rough life of the camp had given her more stamina and strength than the average woman possesses; but even so, she was not far from collapse.

The sun beat fiercely on Conan's tangled black mane. Waves of dizziness and nausea rose in his brain, but he set his teeth and strode on unwaveringly. He was convinced that the city was a reality and not a mirage. What they would find there he had no idea. The inhabitants might be hostile. Nevertheless it was a fighting chance, and that was as much as he had ever asked.

The sun was nigh to setting when they halted in front of the massive gate, grateful for the shade. Conan stood Natala on her feet, and stretched his aching arms. Above them the walls towered some thirty feet in height, composed of a smooth greenish substance that shone almost like glass.

Conan scanned the parapets, expecting to be challenged, but saw no one. Impatiently he shouted, and banged on the gate with his saberhilt, but only the hollow echoes mocked him. Natala cringed close to him, frightened by the silence. Conan tried the portal, and stepped back, drawing his saber, as it swung silently inward. Natala stifled a cry.

"Oh, look, Conan!"

Just inside the gate lay a human body. Conan glared at it narrowly, then looked beyond it. He saw a wide open expanse, like a court, bordered by the arched doorways of houses composed of the same greenish material as the outer walls. These edifices were lofty and imposing, pinnacled with shining domes and minarets. There was no sign of life among them. In the center of the court rose the square curb of a well, and the sight stung Conan, whose mouth felt caked with dry dust. Taking Natala's wrist he drew her through the gate, and closed it behind them.

"Is he dead?" she whispered, shrinkingly indicating the man who lay limply before the gate. The body was that of a tall powerful individual, apparently in his prime; the skin was yellow, the eyes slightly slanted; otherwise the man differed little from the Hyborian type. He was clad in high-strapped sandals and a tunic of purple silk, and a short sword in a cloth-of-gold scabbard hung from his girdle. Conan felt his flesh. It was cold. There was no sign of life in the body.

"Not a wound on him," grunted the Cimmerian, "but he's dead as Almuric with forty Stygian arrows in him. In Crom's name, let's see to the well! If there's water in it, we'll drink, dead men or no."

There was water in the well, but they did not drink of it. Its level was a good fifty feet below the curb, and there was nothing to draw it up with. Conan cursed blackly, maddened by the sight of the stuff just out of his reach, and turned to look for some means of obtaining it. Then a scream from Natala brought him about.

The supposedly dead man was rushing upon him, eyes blazing with indisputable life, his short sword gleaming in his hand. Conan cursed amazedly, but wasted no time in conjecture. He met the hurtling attacker with a slashing cut of his saber that sheared through flesh and bone. The fellow's head thudded on the flags; the body staggered drunkenly, an arch of blood jetting from the severed jugular; then it fell heavily.

Conan glared down, swearing softly.

"This fellow is no deader now than he was a few minutes agone. Into what madhouse have we strayed?"

Natala, who had covered her eyes with her hands at the sight, peeked between her fingers and shook with fear.

"Oh, Conan, will the people of the city not kill us, because of this?"

"Well," he growled, "this creature would have killed us if I hadn't lopped off his head."

He glanced at the archways that gaped blankly from the green walls above them. He saw no hint of movement, heard no sound.

"I don't think any one saw us," he muttered. "I'll hide the evidence—"

He lifted the limp carcass by its swordbelt with one hand, and grasping the head by its long hair in the other, he half carried, half dragged the ghastly remains over to the well.

"Since we can't drink this water," he gritted vindictively, "I'll see that nobody else enjoys drinking it. Curse such a well, anyway!" He heaved the body over the curb and let it drop, tossing the head after it. A dull splash sounded far beneath.

"There's blood on the stones," whispered Natala.

"There'll be more unless I find water soon," growled the Cimmerian, his short store of patience about exhausted. The girl had almost forgotten her thirst and hunger in her fear, but not Conan.

"We'll go into one of these doors," he said. "Surely we'll find people after awhile."

"Oh, Conan!" she wailed, snuggling up as close to him as she could. "I'm afraid! This is a city of ghosts and dead men! Let us go back into the desert! Better to die there, than to face these terrors!"

"We'll go into the desert when they throw us off the walls," he snarled. "There's water somewhere in this city, and I'll find it, if I have to kill every man in it."

"But what if they come to life again?" she whispered.

"Then I'll keep killing them until they stay dead!" he snapped. "Come on! That doorway is as good as another! Stay behind me, but don't run unless I tell you to."

She murmured a faint assent and followed him so closely that she stepped on his heels, to his irritation. Dusk had fallen, filling the strange city with purple shadows. They entered the open doorway, and found themselves in a wide chamber, the walls of which were hung with velvet tapestries, worked in curious designs. Floor, walls and ceiling were of the green glassy stone, the walls decorated with gold frieze-work. Furs and satin cushions littered the floor. Several doorways let into other rooms. They passed through, and traversed several chambers, counterparts of the first. They saw no one, but the Cimmerian grunted suspiciously.

"Some one was here not long ago. This couch is still warm from contact with a human body. That silk cushion bears the imprint of some one's hips. Then there's a faint scent of perfume lingering in the air."

A weird unreal atmosphere hung over all. Traversing this dim silent palace was like an opium dream. Some of the chambers were unlighted, and these they avoided. Others were bathed in a soft weird light that seemed to emanate from jewels set in the walls in fantastic designs. Suddenly, as they passed into one of these illumined chambers, Natala cried out and clutched her companion's arm. With a curse he wheeled, glaring for an enemy, bewildered because he saw none.

"What's the matter?" he snarled. "If you ever grab my swordarm again, I'll skin you. Do you want me to get my throat cut? What were you yelling about?"

"Look there," she quavered, pointing.

Conan grunted. On a table of polished ebony stood golden vessels, apparently containing food and drink. The room was unoccupied.

"Well, whoever this feast is prepared for," he growled, "he'll have to look elsewhere tonight."

"Dare we eat it, Conan?" ventured the girl nervously. "The people might come upon us, and—"

"Lir an mannanan mac lira," he swore, grabbing her by the nape of her neck and thrusting her into a gilded chair at the end of the table with no great ceremony. "We starve and you make objections! Eat!"

He took the chair at the other end, and seizing a jade goblet, emptied it at a gulp. It contained a crimson wine-like liquor of a peculiar tang, unfamiliar to him, but it was like nectar to his parched gullet. His thirst allayed, he attacked the food before him with rare gusto. It too was strange to him: exotic fruits and unknown meats. The vessels were of exquisite workmanship, and there were golden knives and forks as well. These Conan ignored, grasping the meat-joints in his fingers and tearing them with his strong teeth. The Cimmerian's table manners were rather wolfish at any time. His civilized companion ate more daintily, but just as ravenously. It occurred to Conan that the food might be poisoned, but the thought did not lessen his appetite; he preferred to die of poisoning rather than starvation.

His hunger satisfied, he leaned back with a deep sigh of relief. That there were humans in that silent city was evidenced by the fresh food, and perhaps every dark corner concealed a lurking enemy. But he felt no apprehension on that score, having a large confidence in his own fighting ability. He began to feel sleepy, and considered the idea of stretching himself on a near-by couch for a nap.

Not so Natala. She was no longer hungry and thirsty, but she felt no desire to sleep. Her lovely eyes were very wide indeed as she timidly glanced at the doorways, boundaries of the unknown. The silence and mystery of the strange place preyed on her. The chamber seemed larger, the table longer than she had first noticed, and she realized that she was farther from her grim protector than she wished to be. Rising quickly, she went around the table and seated herself on his knee, glancing nervously at the arched doorways.

Some were lighted and some were not, and it was at the unlighted ones she gazed longest.

"We have eaten, drunk and rested," she urged. "Let us leave this place, Conan. It's evil. I can feel it."

"Well, we haven't been harmed so far," he began, when a soft but sinister rustling brought him about. Thrusting the girl off his knee he rose with the quick ease of a panther, drawing his saber, facing the doorway from which the sound had seemed to come. It was not repeated, and he stole forward noiselessly, Natala following with her heart in her mouth. She knew he suspected peril. His outthrust head was sunk between his giant shoulders, he glided forward in a half crouch, like a stalking tiger. He made no more noise than a tiger would have made.

At the doorway he halted, Natala peering fearfully from behind him. There was no light in the room, but it was partially illuminated by the radiance behind them, which streamed across it into yet another chamber. And in this chamber a man lay on a raised dais. The soft light bathed him, and they saw he was a counterpart of the man Conan had killed before the outer gate, except that his garments were richer, and ornamented with jewels which twinkled in the uncanny light. Was he dead, or merely sleeping? Again came that faint sinister sound, as if some one had thrust aside a hanging. Conan drew back, drawing the clinging

Natala with him. He clapped his hand over her mouth just in time to check her shriek.

From where they now stood, they could no longer see the dais, but they could see the shadow it cast on the wall behind it. And now another shadow moved across the wall: a huge shapeless black blot. Conan felt his hair prickle curiously as he watched. Distorted though it might be, he felt that he had never seen a man or beast which cast such a shadow. He was consumed with curiosity, but some instinct held him frozen in his tracks. He heard Natala's quick panting gasps as she stared with dilated eyes. No other sound disturbed the tense stillness. The great shadow engulfed that of the dais. For a long instant only its black bulk was thrown on the smooth wall. Then slowly it receded, and once more the dais was etched darkly against the wall. But the sleeper was no longer upon it.

An hysterical gurgle rose in Natala's throat, and Conan gave her an admonitory shake. He was aware of an iciness in his own veins. Human foes he did not fear; anything understandable, however grisly, caused no tremors in his broad breast. But this was beyond his ken.

After a while, however, his curiosity conquered his uneasiness, and he moved out into the unlighted chamber again, ready for anything. Looking into the other room, he saw it was empty. The dais stood as he had first seen it, except that no bejeweled human lay thereon. Only on its silken covering shone a single drop of blood, like a great crimson gem. Natala saw it and gave a low choking cry, for which Conan did not punish her. Again he felt the icy hand of fear. On that dais a man had lain; something had crept into the chamber and carried him away. What that something was, Conan had no idea, but an aura of unnatural horror hung over those dim-lit chambers.

He was ready to depart. Taking Natala's hand, he turned back, then hesitated. Somewhere back among the chambers they had traversed, he heard the sound of a footfall. A human foot, bare or softly shod, had made that sound, and Conan, with the wariness of a wolf, turned quickly aside. He believed he could come again into the outer court, and yet avoid the room from which the sound had appeared to come.

But they had not crossed the first chamber on their new route, when the rustle of a silken hanging brought them about suddenly. Before a curtained alcove stood a man eyeing them intently.

He was exactly like the others they had encountered: tall, well made, clad in purple garments, with a jeweled girdle. There was neither surprise nor hostility in his amber eyes. They were dreamy as a lotus-eater's. He did not draw the short sword at his side. After a tense moment he spoke, in a far-away detached tone, and a language his hearers did not understand.

On a venture Conan replied in Stygian, and the stranger answered in the same tongue: "Who are you?"

"I am Conan, a Cimmerian," answered the barbarian. "This is Natala, of Brythunia. What city is this?"

The man did not at once reply. His dreamy sensuous gaze rested on Natala, and he drawled, "Of all my rich visions, this is the strangest! Oh, girl of the golden locks, from what far dreamland do you come? From Andarra, or Tothra, or Kuth of the star-girdle?"

"What madness is this?" growled the Cimmerian harshly, not relishing the man's words or manner.

The other did not heed him.

"I have dreamed more gorgeous beauties," he murmured; "lithe women with hair dusky as night, and dark eyes of unfathomed mystery. But your skin is white as milk, your eyes as clear as dawn, and there is about you a freshness and daintiness alluring as honey. Come to my couch, little dream-girl!"

He advanced and reached for her, and Conan struck aside his hand with a force that might have broken his arm. The man reeled back, clutching the numbed member, his eyes clouding.

"What rebellion of ghosts is this?" he muttered. "Barbarian, I command ye—begone! Fade! Dissipate! Fade! Vanish!"

"I'll vanish your head from your shoulders!" snarled the infuriated Cimmerian, his saber gleaming in his hand. "Is this the welcome you give strangers? By Crom, I'll drench these hangings in blood!"

The dreaminess had faded from the other's eyes, to be replaced by a look of bewilderment.

"Thog!" he ejaculated. "You are real! Whence come you? Who are you? What do you in Xuthal?"

"We came from the desert," Conan growled. "We wandered into the city at dusk, famishing. We found a feast set for some one, and we ate it. I have no money to pay for it. In my country, no starving man is denied food, but you civilized people must have your recompense—if you are like all I ever met. We have done no harm and we were just leaving. By Crom, I do not like this place, where dead men rise, and sleeping men vanish into the bellies of shadows!"

The man started violently at the last comment, his yellow face turning ashy.

"What do you say? Shadows? Into the bellies of shadows?"

"Well," answered the Cimmerian cautiously, "whatever it is that takes a man from a sleeping-dais and leaves only a spot of blood."

"You have seen? You have seen?" The man was shaking like a leaf; his voice cracked on the high-pitched note.

"Only a man sleeping on a dais, and a shadow that engulfed him," answered Conan.

The effect of his words on the other was horrifying. With an awful scream the man turned and rushed from the chamber. In his blind haste he caromed from the side of the door, righted himself, and fled through the adjoining chambers, still screaming at the top of his voice. Amazed, Conan stared after him, the girl trembling as she clutched the giant's arm. They could no longer see the flying figure, but they still heard his frightful screams, dwindling in the distance, and echoing as from vaulted roofs. Suddenly one cry, louder than the others, rose and broke short, followed by blank silence.

"Crom!"

Conan wiped the perspiration from his forehead with a hand that was not entirely steady.

"Surely this is a city of the mad! Let's get out of here, before we meet other madmen!"

"It is all a nightmare!" whimpered Natala. "We are dead and damned! We died out on the desert and are in hell! We are disembodied spirits—ow!" Her yelp was induced by a resounding spank from Conan's open hand.

"You're no spirit when a pat makes you yell like that," he commented, with the grim humor which frequently manifested itself at inopportune times. "We are alive,

19

though we may not be if we loiter in this devil-haunted pile. Come!"

They had traversed but a single chamber when again they stopped short. Some one or something was approaching. They faced the doorway whence the sounds came, waiting for they knew not what. Conan's nostrils widened, and his eyes narrowed. He caught the faint scent of the perfume he had noticed earlier in the night. A figure framed itself in the doorway. Conan swore under his breath; Natala's red lips opened wide.

It was a woman who stood there staring at them in wonder. She was tall, lithe, shaped like a goddess; clad in a narrow girdle crusted with jewels. A burnished mass of night-black hair set off the whiteness of her ivory body. Her dark eyes, shaded by long dusky lashes, were deep with sensuous mystery. Conan caught his breath at her beauty, and Natala stared with dilated eyes. The Cimmerian had never seen such a woman; her facial outline was Stygian, but she was not dusky-skinned like the Stygian women he had known; her limbs were like alabaster.

But when she spoke, in a deep rich musical voice, it was in the Stygian tongue.

"Who are you? What do you in Xuthal? Who is that girl?"

"Who are you?" bluntly countered Conan, who quickly wearied of answering questions.

"I am Thalis the Stygian," she replied. "Are you mad, to come here?"

"I've been thinking I must be," he growled. "By Crom, if I am sane, I'm out of place here, because these people are all maniacs. We stagger in from the desert, dying of thirst and hunger, and we come upon a dead man who tries to stab me in the back. We enter a palace rich and luxuriant, yet apparently empty. We find a meal set, but with no feasters. Then we see a shadow devour a sleeping man—" He watched her narrowly and saw her change color slightly. "Well?"

"Well what?" she demanded, apparently regaining control of herself.

"I was just waiting for you to run through the rooms howling like a wild woman," he answered. "The man I told about the shadow did."

She shrugged her slim ivory shoulders. "That was the screams I heard, then. Well, to every man his fate, and it's foolish to squeal like a rat in a trap. When Thog wants me, he will come for me."

"Who is Thog?" demanded Conan suspiciously.

She gave him a long appraising stare that brought color to Natala's face and made her bite her small red lip.

"Sit down on that divan and I will tell you," she said. "But first tell me your names."

"I am Conan, a Cimmerian, and this is Natala, a daughter of Brythunia," he answered. "We are refugees of an army destroyed on the borders of Kush. But I am not desirous of sitting down, where black shadows might steal up on my back."

With a light musical laugh, she seated herself, stretching out her supple limbs with studied abandon.

"Be at ease," she advised. "If Thog wishes you, he will take you, wherever you are. That man you mentioned, who screamed and ran—did you not hear him give one great cry, and then fall silent? In his frenzy, he must have run full into that which he sought to escape. No man can avoid his fate."

Conan grunted non-committally, but he sat down on the edge of a couch, his saber across his knees, his eyes wandering suspiciously about the chamber. Natala nestled against him, clutching him jealously, her legs tucked up under her. She eyed the stranger woman with suspicion and resentment. She felt small and dust-stained and insignificant before this glamorous beauty, and she could not mistake the look in the dark eyes which feasted on every detail of the bronzed giant's physique.

"What is this place, and who are these people?" demanded Conan.

"This city is called Xuthal; it is very ancient. It is built over an oasis, which the founders of Xuthal found in their wanderings.

They came from the east, so long ago that not even their descendants remember the age.

"Surely there are not many of them; these palaces seem empty."

"No; and yet more than you might think. The city is really one great palace, with every building inside the walls closely connected with the others. You might walk among these chambers for hours and see no one. At other times, you would meet hundreds of the inhabitants."

"How is that?" Conan inquired uneasily; this savored too strongly of sorcery for comfort.

"Much of the time these people lie in sleep. Their dream-life is as important—and to them as real—as their waking life. You have heard of the black lotus? In certain pits of the city it grows. Through the ages they have cultivated it, until, instead of death, its juice induces dreams, gorgeous and fantastic. In these dreams they spend most of their time. Their lives are vague, erratic, and without plan. They dream, they wake, drink, love, eat and dream again. They seldom finish anything they begin, but leave it half completed and sink back again into the slumber of the black lotus. That meal you found—doubtless one awoke, felt the urge of hunger, prepared the meal for himself, then forgot about it and wandered away to dream again."

"Where do they get their food?" interrupted Conan. "I saw no fields or vineyards outside the city. Have they orchards and cattle-pens within the walls?"

She shook her head. "They manufacture their own food out of the primal elements. They are wonderful scientists, when they are not drugged with their dream-flower. Their ancestors were mental giants, who built this marvelous city in the desert, and though the race became slaves to their curious passions, some of their wonderful knowledge still remains. Have you wondered about these lights? They are jewels, fused with radium. You rub them with your thumb to make them glow, and rub them again, the opposite way, to extinguish them. That is but a single example of their science. But much they have forgotten. They take little interest in waking life, choosing to lie most of the time in death-like sleep."

"Then the dead man at the gate—" began Conan.

"Was doubtless slumbering. Sleepers of the lotus are like the dead. Animation is apparently suspended. It is impossible to detect the slightest sign of life. The spirit has left the body and is roaming at will through other, exotic worlds. The man at the gate was a good example of the irresponsibility of these people's lives. He was guarding the gate, where custom decrees a watch be kept, though no enemy has ever advanced across the desert. In other parts of the city you would find other guards, generally sleeping as soundly as the man at the gate."

Conan mulled over this for a space.

"Where are the people now?"

"Scattered in different parts of the city; lying on couches, on silken divans, in cushion-littered alcoves, on fur-covered daises; all wrapt in the shining veil of dreams."

Conan felt the skin twitch between his massive shoulders. It was not soothing to think of hundreds of people lying cold and still throughout the tapestried palaces, their glassy eyes turned unseeingly upward. He remembered something else.

"What of the thing that stole through the chambers and carried away the man on the dais?"

A shudder twitched her ivory limbs.

"That was Thog, the Ancient, the god of Xuthal, who dwells in the sunken dome in the center of the city. He has always dwelt in Xuthal. Whether he came here with the ancient founders, or was here when they built the city, none knows. But the people of Xuthal worship him. Mostly he sleeps below the city, but sometimes at irregular intervals he grows hungry, and then he steals through the secret corridors and the dim-lit chambers, seeking prey. Then none is safe."

Natala moaned with terror and clasped Conan's mighty neck as if to resist an effort to drag her from her protector's side.

"Crom!" he ejaculated aghast. "You mean to tell me these people lie down calmly and sleep, with this demon crawling among them?"

"It is only occasionally that he is hungry," she repeated. "A god must have his sacrifices. When I was a child in Stygia the people lived under the shadow of the priests. None ever knew when he or she would be seized and dragged to the altar. What difference whether the priests give a victim to the gods, or the god comes for his own victim?"

"Such is not the custom of my people," Conan growled, "nor of Natala's either. The Hyborians do not sacrifice humans to their god, Mitra, and as for my people—by Crom, I'd like to see a priest try to drag a Cimmerian to the altar! There'd be blood spilt, but not as the priest intended."

"You are a barbarian," laughed Thalis, but with a glow in her luminous eyes. "Thog is very ancient and very terrible."

"These folk must be either fools or heroes," grunted Conan, "to lie down and dream their idiotic dreams, knowing they might awaken in his belly."

She laughed. "They know nothing else. For untold generations Thog has preyed on them. He has been one of the factors which have reduced their numbers from thousands to hundreds. A few more generations and they will be extinct, and Thog must either fare forth into the world for new prey, or retire to the underworld whence he came so long ago.

"They realize their ultimate doom, but they are fatalists, incapable of resistance or escape. Not one of the present generation has been out of sight of these walls. There is an oasis a day's march to the south—I have seen it on the old maps their ancestors drew on parchment—but no man of Xuthal has visited it for three generations, much less made any attempt to explore the fertile grasslands which the maps show lying another day's march beyond it. They are a fast-fading race, drowned in lotus dreams, stimulating their waking hours by means of the golden wine which heals wounds, prolongs life, and invigorates the most sated debauchee.

"Yet they cling to life, and fear the deity they worship. You saw how one went mad at the knowledge that Thog was roving the palaces. I have seen the whole city screaming and tearing its hair, and running frenziedly out of the gates, to cower outside the walls and draw lots to see which would be bound and flung back through the arched doorways to satisfy Thog's lust and hunger. Were they not all slumbering now, the word of his coming would send them raving and shrieking again through the outer gates."

"Oh, Conan!" begged Natala hysterically. "Let us flee!"

"In good time," muttered Conan, his eyes burning on Thalis ivory limbs. "What are you, a Stygian woman, doing here?"

"I came here when a young girl," she answered, leaning lithely back against the velvet divan, and intertwining her slender fingers behind her dusky head. "I am the daughter of a king, no common woman, as you can see by my skin, which is as white as that of your little blond there. I was abducted by a rebel prince, who, with an army of Kushite bowmen, pushed southward into the wilderness, searching for a land he could make his own. He and all his warriors perished in the desert, but one, before he died, placed me on a camel and walked beside it until he dropped and died in his tracks. The beast wandered on, and I finally passed into delirium from thirst and hunger, and awakened in this city. They told me I had been seen from the walls, early in the dawn, lying senseless beside a dead camel. They went forth and brought me in and revived me with their wonderful golden wine. And only the sight of a woman would have led them to have ventured that far from their walls.

"They were naturally much interested in me, especially the men. As I could not speak their language, they learned to speak mine. They are very quick and able of intellect; they learned my language long before I learned theirs. But they were more interested in me than in my language. I have been, and am, the only thing for which a man of them will forgo his lotus-dreams for a space."

She laughed wickedly, flashing her audacious eyes meaningly at Conan.

"Of course the women are jealous of me," she continued tranquilly. "They are handsome enough in their yellow-skinned way, but they are dreamy and uncertain as the men, and these latter like me not only for my beauty, but for my reality. I am no dream! Though I have dreamed the dreams of the lotus, I am a normal woman, with earthly emotions and desires. With such these moon-eyed yellow women can not compare.

"That is why it would be better for you to cut that girl's throat with your saber, before the men of Xuthal waken and catch her. They will put her through paces she never dreamed of! She is too soft to endure what I have thrived on. I am a daughter of Luxur, and before I had known fifteen summers I had been led through the temples of Derketo, the dusky goddess, and had been initiated into the mysteries. Not that my first years in Xuthal were years of unmodified pleasure! The people of Xuthal have forgotten more than the priestesses of Derketo ever dreamed. They live only for sensual joys. Dreaming or waking, their lives are filled with exotic ecstasies, beyond the ken of ordinary men."

"Damned degenerates!" growled Conan.

"It is all in the point of view," smiled Thalis lazily.

"Well," he decided, "we're merely wasting time. I can see this is no place for ordinary mortals. We'll be gone before your morons awake, or Thog comes to devour us. I think the desert would be kinder."

Natala, whose blood had curdled in her veins at Thalis's words, fervently agreed. She could speak Stygian only brokenly, but she understood it well enough. Conan stood up, drawing her up beside him.

"If you'll show us the nearest way out of this city," he grunted, "we'll take ourselves off." But his gaze lingered on the Stygian's sleek limbs and ivory breasts.

She did not miss his look, and she smiled enigmatically as she rose with the lithe ease of a great lazy cat.

"Follow me," she directed and led the way, conscious of Conan's eyes fixed on her supple figure and perfectly poised carriage. She did not go the way they had come, but before Conan's suspicions could be roused, she halted in a wide ivory-cased chamber, and pointed to a tiny fountain which gurgled in the center of the ivory floor.

"Don't you want to wash your face, child?" she asked Natala. "It is stained with dust, and there is dust in your hair."

Natala colored resentfully at the suggestion of malice in the Stygian's faintly mocking tone, but she complied, wondering miserably just how much havoc the desert sun and wind had wrought on her complexion—a feature for which women of her race were justly noted. She knelt beside the fountain, shook back her hair, slipped her tunic down to her waist, and began to lave not only her face, but her white arms and shoulders as well.

"By Crom!" grumbled Conan. "A woman will stop to consider her beauty, if the devil himself were on her heels. Haste, girl; you'll be dusty again before we've got out of sight of this city. And Thalis, I'd take it kindly if you'd furnish us with a bit of food and drink."

For answer Thalis leaned herself against him, slipping one white arm about his bronzed shoulders. Her sleek naked flank pressed against his thigh and the perfume of her foamy hair was in his nostrils.

"Why dare the desert?" she whispered urgently. "Stay here! I will teach you the ways of Xuthal. I will protect you. I will love you! You are a real man: I am sick of these mooncalves who sigh and dream and wake, and dream again. I am hungry for the hard, clean passion of a man from the earth. The blaze of your dynamic eyes makes my heart pound in my bosom, and the touch of your iron-thewed arm maddens me.

"Stay here! I will make you king of Xuthal! I will show you all the ancient mysteries, and the exotic ways of pleasure! I—" She had thrown both arms about his neck and was standing on tiptoe, her vibrant body shivering against his. Over her ivory shoulder he saw Natala, throwing back her damp tousled hair, stop short, her lovely eyes dilating, her red lips parting in a shocked O. With an embarrassed grunt, Conan disengaged Thalis's clinging arms and put her aside with one massive arm. She threw a swift glance at the

Brythunian girl and smiled enigmatically, seeming to nod her splendid head in mysterious cogitation.

Natala rose and jerked up her tunic, her eyes blazing, her lips pouting sulkily. Conan swore under his breath. He was no more monogamous in his nature than the average soldier of fortune, but there was an innate decency about him that was Natala's best protection.

Thalis did not press her suit. Beckoning them with her slender hand to follow, she turned and walked across the chamber.

There, close to the tapestried wall, she halted suddenly. Conan, watching her, wondered if she had heard the sounds that might be made by a nameless monster stealing through the midnight chambers, and his skin crawled at the thought.

"What do you hear?" he demanded.

"Watch that doorway," she replied, pointing.

He wheeled, sword ready. Only the empty arch of the entrance met his gaze. Then behind him sounded a quick faint scuffling noise, a half-choked gasp. He whirled. Thalis and Natala had vanished. The tapestry was settling back in place, as if it had been lifted away from the wall. As he gaped bewilderedly, from behind that tapestried wall rang a muffled scream in the voice of the Brythunian girl.

CHAPTER II

When Conan turned, in compliance with Thalis's request, to glare at the doorway opposite, Natala had been standing just behind him, close to the side of the Stygian. The instant the Cimmerian's back was turned, Thalis, with a pantherish quickness almost incredible, clapped her hand over Natala's mouth, stifling the cry she tried to give. Simultaneously the Stygian's other arm was passed about the blond girl's supple waist, and she was jerked back against the wall, which seemed to give way as Thalis" shoulder pressed against it. A section of the wall swung inward, and through a slit that opened in the tapestry Thalis slid with her captive, just as Conan wheeled back.

Inside was utter blackness as the secret door swung to again. Thalis paused to fumble at it for an instant, apparently sliding home a bolt, and as she took her hand from Natala's mouth to perform this act, the Brythunian girl began to scream at the top of her voice. Thalis's laugh was like poisoned honey in the darkness.

"Scream if you will, little fool. It will only shorten your life."

At that Natala ceased suddenly, and cowered shaking in every limb.

"Why did you do this?" she begged. "What are you going to do?"

"I am going to take you down this corridor for a short distance," answered Thalis, "and leave you for one who will sooner or later come for you."

"Ohhhhhh!" Natala's voice broke in a sob of terror. "Why should you harm me? I have never injured you!"

"I want your warrior. You stand in my way. He desires me—I could read the look in his eyes. But for you, he would be willing to stay here and be my king. When you are out of the way, he will follow me."

"He will cut your throat," answered Natala with conviction, knowing Conan better than Thalis did.

"We shall see," answered the Stygian coolly from the confidence of her power over men. "At any rate, you will not know whether he stabs or kisses me, because you will be the bride of him who dwells in darkness. Come!"

Half mad with terror, Natala fought like a wild thing, but it availed her nothing. With a lithe strength she would not have believed possible in a woman, Thalis picked her up and carried her down the black corridor as if she had been a child. Natala did not scream again, remembering the Stygian's sinister words; the only sounds were her desperate quick panting and Thalis" soft taunting lascivious laughter. Then the Brythunian's fluttering hand closed on something in the dark—a jeweled dagger-hilt jutting from Thalis's gem-crusted girdle. Natala jerked it forth and struck blindly and with all her girlish power.

A scream burst from Thalis's lips, feline in its pain and fury. She reeled, and Natala slipped from her relaxing grasp, to bruise her tender limbs on the smooth stone floor. Rising, she scurried to the nearest wall and stood there panting and trembling, flattening herself against the stones. She could not see Thalis, but she could hear her. The Stygian was quite certainly not dead. She was cursing in a steady stream, and her fury was so concentrated and deadly that Natala felt her bones turn to wax, her blood to ice.

"Where are you, you little she-devil?" gasped Thalis. "Let me get my fingers on you again, and I'll—" Natala grew physically sick as Thalis described the bodily injuries she intended to inflict on her rival. The Stygian's choice of language would have shamed the toughest courtezan in Aquilonia.

Natala heard her groping in the dark, and then a light sprang up. Evidently whatever fear Thalis felt of the black corridor was submerged in her anger. The light came from one of the radium gems which adorned the walls of Xuthal. This Thalis had rubbed, and now she stood bathed in its reddish glow: a light different from that which the others had emitted. One hand was pressed to her side and blood trickled between the fingers. But she did not seem weakened or badly hurt, and her eyes blazed fiendishly. What little courage remained to Natala ebbed away at sight of the Stygian standing limned in that weird glow, her beautiful face contorted with a passion that was no less than hellish. She now advanced with a pantherish tread, drawing her hand away from her wounded side, and shaking the blood drops impatiently from her fingers. Natala saw that she had not badly harmed her rival. The blade had glanced from the jewels of Thalis's girdle and inflicted only a very superficial flesh-wound, only enough to rouse the Stygian's unbridled fury.

"Give me that dagger, you fool!" she gritted, striding up to the cowering girl.

Natala knew she ought to fight while she had the chance, but she simply could not summon up the courage. Never much of a fighter, the darkness, violence and horror of her adventure had left her limp, mentally and physically. Thalis snatched the dagger from her lax fingers and threw it contemptuously aside.

"You little slut!" she ground between her teeth, slapping the girl viciously with either hand. "Before I drag you down the corridor and throw you into Thog's jaws I'll have a little of your blood myself! You would dare to knife me—well, for that audacity you shall pay!"

Seizing her by the hair, Thalis dragged her down the corridor a short distance, to the edge of the circle of light. A metal ring showed in the wall, above the level of a man's head. From it depended a silken cord. As in a nightmare Natala felt her tunic being stripped from her, and the next instant Thalis had jerked up her wrists and bound them to the ring, where she hung, naked as the day she was born, her feet barely touching the floor. Twisting her head, Natala saw Thalis unhook a jewel-handled whip from where it hung on the wall, near the ring. The lashes consisted of seven round silk cords, harder yet more pliant than leather thongs.

With a hiss of vindictive gratification, Thalis drew back her arm, and Natala shrieked as the cords curled across her loins. The tortured girl writhed, twisted and tore agonizedly at the thongs which imprisoned her wrists. She had forgotten the lurking menace her cries might summon, and so apparently had Thalis. Every stroke evoked screams of anguish. The whippings Natala had received in the Shemite slave-markets paled to insignificance before this. She had never guessed the punishing power of hard-woven silk cords. Their caress was more exquisitely painful than any birch twigs or leather thongs. They whistled venomously as they cut the air.

Then, as Natala twisted her tear-stained face over her shoulder to shriek for mercy, something froze her cries. Agony gave place to paralyzing horror in her beautiful eyes.

Struck by her expression, Thalis checked her lifted hand and whirled quick as a cat. Too late! An awful cry rang from her lips as she swayed back, her arms upflung. Natala saw her for an instant, a white figure of fear etched against a great black shapeless mass that towered over her; then the white figure was whipped off its feet, the shadow receded with it, and in the circle of dim light Natala hung alone, half fainting with terror.

From the black shadows came sounds, incomprehensible and blood-freezing. She heard Thalis's voice pleading frenziedly, but no voice answered. There was no sound except the Stygian's panting voice, which suddenly rose to screams of agony, and then broke in hysterical laughter, mingled with sobs. This dwindled to a convulsive panting, and presently this too ceased, and a silence more terrible hovered over the secret corridor.

Nauseated with horror, Natala twisted about and dared to look fearfully in the direction the black shape had carried Thalis. She saw nothing, but she sensed an unseen peril, more grisly than she could understand. She fought against a rising tide of hysteria. Her bruised wrists, her smarting body were forgotten in the teeth of this menace which she dimly felt threatened not only her body, but her soul as well.

She strained her eyes into the blackness beyond the rim of the dim light, tense with fear of what she might see. A whimpering gasp escaped her lips. The darkness was taking form. Something huge and bulky grew up out of the void. She saw a great misshapen head emerging into the light. At least she took it for a head, though it was not the member of any sane or normal creature. She saw a great toad-like face, the features of which were as dim and unstable as those of a specter seen in a mirror of nightmare. Great pools of light that might have been eyes blinked at her, and she shook at the cosmic lust reflected there. She could tell nothing about the creature's body. Its outline seemed to waver and alter subtly even as she looked at it; yet its substance was apparently solid enough. There was nothing misty or ghostly about it.

As it came toward her, she could not tell whether it walked, wriggled, flew or crept. Its method of locomotion was absolutely beyond her comprehension. When it had emerged from the shadows she was still uncertain as to its nature. The light from the radium gem did not illumine it as it would have illumined an ordinary creature. Impossible as it seemed, the being seemed almost impervious to the light. Its details were still obscure and indistinct, even when it halted so near that it almost touched her shrinking flesh. Only the blinking toad-like face stood out with any distinctness. The thing was a blur in the sight, a black blot of shadow that normal radiance would neither dissipate nor illuminate.

She decided she was mad, because she could not tell whether the being looked up at her or towered above her. She was unable to say whether the dim repulsive face blinked up at her from the shadows at her feet, or looked down at her from an immense height. But if her sight convinced her that whatever its mutable qualities, it was yet composed of solid substance, her sense of feel further assured her of that fact. A dark tentacle-like member slid about her body, and she screamed at the touch of it on her naked flesh. It was neither warm nor cold, rough nor smooth; it was like nothing that had ever touched her before, and at its caress she knew such fear and shame as she had never dreamed of. All the obscenity and salacious infamy spawned in the muck of the abysmal pits of Life seemed to drown her in seas of cosmic filth. And in that instant she knew that whatever form of life this thing represented it was not a beast.

She began to scream uncontrollably, the monster tugged at her as if to tear her from the ring by sheer brutality; then something crashed above their heads, and a form hurtled down through the air to strike the stone floor.

CHAPTER III

When Conan wheeled to see the tapestry settling back in place and to hear Natala's muffled cry, he hurled himself against the wall with a maddened roar. Rebounding from the impact that would have splintered the bones of a lesser man, he ripped away the tapestry revealing what appeared to be a blank wall. Beside himself with fury he lifted his saber as though to hew through the marble, when a sudden sound brought him about, eyes blazing.

A score of figures faced him, yellow men in purple tunics, with short swords in their hands. As he turned they surged in on him with hostile cries. He made no attempt to conciliate them. Maddened at the disappearance of his sweetheart, the barbarian reverted to type.

A snarl of bloodthirsty gratification hummed in his bull-throat as he leaped, and the first attacker, his short sword overreached by the whistling saber, went down with his brains gushing from his split skull. Wheeling like a cat, Conan caught a descending wrist on his edge, and the hand gripping the short sword flew into the air scattering a shower of red drops. But Conan had not paused or hesitated. A pantherish twist and shift of his body avoided the blundering rush of two yellow swordsmen, and the blade of one missing its objective, was sheathed in the breast of the other.

A yell of dismay went up at this mischance, and Conan allowed himself a short bark of laughter as he bounded aside from a whistling cut and slashed under the guard of yet another man of Xuthal. A long spurt of crimson followed his singing edge and the man crumpled screaming, his belly-muscles cut through.

The warriors of Xuthal howled like mad wolves. Unaccustomed to battle, they were ridiculously slow and clumsy compared to the tigerish barbarian whose motions were blurs of quickness possible only to steel thews knit to a perfect fighting brain. They floundered and stumbled, hindered by their own numbers; they struck too quick or too soon, and cut only empty air. He was never motionless or in the same place an instant; springing, side-stepping, whirling, twisting, he offered a constantly shifting target for their swords, while his own curved blade sang death about their ears.

But whatever their faults, the men of Xuthal did not lack courage. They swarmed about him yelling and hacking, and through the arched doorways rushed others, awakened from their slumbers by the unwonted clamor.

Conan, bleeding from a cut on the temple, cleared a space for an instant with a devastating sweep of his dripping saber, and cast a quick glance about for an avenue of escape. At that instant he saw the tapestry on one of the walls drawn aside, disclosing a narrow stairway. On this stood a man in rich robes, vague-eyed and blinking, as if he had just awakened and had not yet shaken the dusts of slumber from his brain. Conan's sight and action were simultaneous.

A tigerish leap carried him untouched through the hemming ring of swords, and he bounded toward the stair with the pack giving tongue behind him. Three men confronted him at the foot of the marble steps, and he struck them with a deafening crash of steel. There was a frenzied instant when the blades flamed like summer lightning; then the group fell apart and Conan sprang up the stair. The oncoming horde tripped over three writhing forms at its foot: one lay face-down in a sickening welter of blood and brains; another propped himself on his hands, blood spurting blackly from his severed throat veins; the other howled like a dying dog as he clawed at the crimson stump that had been an arm.

As Conan rushed up the marble stair, the man above shook himself from his stupor and drew a sword that sparkled frostily in the radium light. He thrust downward as the barbarian surged upon him. But as the point sang toward his throat, Conan ducked deeply. The blade slit the skin of his back, and Conan straightened, driving his saber upward as a man might wield a butcher-knife, with all the power of his mighty shoulders.

So terrific was his headlong drive that the sinking of the saber to the hilt into the belly of his enemy did not check him. He caromed against the wretch's body, knocking it sideways. The impact sent Conan crashing against the wall; the other, the saber torn through his body, fell headlong down the stair, ripped open to the spine from groin to broken breastbone. In a ghastly mess of streaming entrails the body tumbled against the men rushing up the stairs, bearing them back with it.

Half stunned, Conan leaned against the wall an instant, glaring down upon them; then with a defiant shake of his dripping saber, he bounded up the steps.

Coming into an upper chamber, he halted only long enough to see that it was empty. Behind him the horde was yelling with such intensified horror and rage, that he knew he had killed some notable man there on the stair, probably the king of that fantastic city.

He ran at random, without plan. He desperately wished to find and succor Natala, who he was sure needed aid badly; but harried as he was by all the warriors in Xuthal, he could only run on, trusting to luck to elude them and find her. Among those dark or dimly lighted upper chambers he quickly lost all sense of direction, and it was not strange that he eventually blundered into a chamber into which his foes were just pouring.

They yelled vengefully and rushed for him, and with a snarl of disgust he turned and fled back the way he had come. At least he thought it was the way he had come. But presently, racing into a particularly ornate chamber, he was aware of his mistake. All the chambers he had traversed since mounting the stair had been empty. This chamber had an occupant, who rose up with a cry as he charged in.

Conan saw a yellow-skinned woman, loaded with jeweled ornaments but otherwise nude, staring at him with wide eyes. So much he glimpsed as she raised her hand and jerked a silken rope hanging from the wall. Then the floor dropped from under him, and all his steel-trap coordination could not save him from the plunge into the black depths that opened beneath him.

He did not fall any great distance, though it was far enough to have snapped the leg bones of a man not built of steel springs and whalebone.

He hit cat-like on his feet and one hand, instinctively retaining his grasp on his saber hilt. A familiar cry rang in his ears as he rebounded on his feet as a lynx rebounds with snarling bared fangs. So Conan, glaring from under his tousled mane, saw the white naked figure of Natala writhing in the lustful grasp of a black nightmare shape that could have only been bred in the lost pits of hell.

The sight of that awful shape alone might have frozen the Cimmerian with fear. In juxtaposition to his girl, the sight sent a red wave of murderous fury through Conan's brain. In a crimson mist he smote the monster.

It dropped the girl, wheeling toward its attacker, and the maddened Cimmerian's saber, shrilling through the air, sheared clear through the black viscous bulk and rang on the stone floor, showering blue sparks. Conan went to his knees from the fury of the blow; the edge had not encountered the resistance he had expected. As he bounded up, the thing was upon him.

It towered above him like a clinging black cloud. It seemed to flow about him in almost liquid waves, to envelop and engulf him. His madly slashing saber sheared through it again and again, his ripping poniard tore and rent it; he was deluged with a slimy liquid that must have been its sluggish blood. Yet its fury was nowise abated.

He could not tell whether he was slashing off its members or whether he was cleaving its bulk, which knit behind the slicing blade. He was tossed to and fro in the violence of that awful battle, and had a dazed feeling that he was fighting not one, but an aggregation of lethal creatures. The thing seemed to be biting, clawing, crushing and clubbing him all at the same time. He felt fangs and talons rend his flesh; flabby cables that were yet hard as iron encircled his limbs and body, and worse than all, something like a whip of scorpions fell again and again across his shoulders, back and breast, tearing the skin and filling his veins with a poison that was like liquid fire.

They had rolled beyond the circle of light, and it was in utter blackness that the Cimmerian battled. Once he sank his teeth, beast-like, into the flabby substance of his foe, revolting as the stuff writhed and squirmed like living rubber from between his iron jaws.

In that hurricane of battle they were rolling over and over, farther and farther down the tunnel. Conan's brain reeled with the punishment he was taking. His breath came in whistling gasps between his teeth. High above him he saw a great toadlike face, dimly limned in an eery glow that seemed to emanate from it. And with a panting cry that was half curse, half gasp of straining agony, he lunged toward it, thrusting with all his waning power. Hilt-deep the saber sank, somewhere below the grisly face, and a convulsive shudder heaved the vast bulk that half enveloped the Cimmerian. With a volcanic burst of contraction and expansion, it tumbled backward, rolling now with frantic haste down the corridor. Conan went with it, bruised, battered, invincible, hanging on like a bulldog to the hilt of his saber which he could not withdraw, tearing and ripping at the shuddering bulk with the poniard in his left hand, goring it to ribbons.

The thing glowed all over now with a weird phosphorous radiance, and this glow was in Conan's eyes, blinding him, as suddenly the heaving billowing mass fell away from beneath him, the saber tearing loose and remaining in his locked hand. This hand and arm hung down into space, and far below him the glowing body of the monster was rushing downward like a meteor. Conan dazedly realized that he lay on the brink of a great round well, the edge of which was slimy stone. He lay there watching the hurtling glow dwindling and dwindling until it vanished into a dark shining surface that seemed to surge upward to meet it. For an instant a dimming witchfire glimmered in those dusky depths; then it disappeared and Conan lay staring down into the blackness of the ultimate abyss from which no sound came.

CHAPTER IV

Straining vainly at the silk cords which cut into her wrists, Natala sought to pierce the darkness beyond the radiant circle. Her tongue seemed frozen to the roof of her mouth. Into that blackness she had seen Conan vanish, locked in mortal combat with the unknown demon, and the only sounds that had come to her straining ears had been the panting gasps of the barbarian, the impact of struggling bodies, and the thud and rip of savage blows. These ceased, and Natala swayed dizzily on her cords, half fainting.

A footstep roused her out of her apathy of horror, to see Conan emerging from the darkness. At the sight she found her voice in a shriek which echoed down the vaulted tunnel. The manhandling the Cimmerian had received was appalling to behold. At every step he dripped blood. His face was skinned and bruised as if he had been beaten with a bludgeon. His lips were pulped, and blood oozed down his face from a wound in his scalp. There were deep gashes in his thighs, calves and forearms, and great bruises showed on his limbs and body from impacts against the stone floor. But his shoulders, back and upper-breast muscles had suffered most. The flesh was bruised, swollen and lacerated, the skin hanging in loose strips, as if he had been lashed with wire whips.

"Oh, Conan!" she sobbed. "What has happened to you?"

He had no breath for conversation, but his smashed lips writhed in what might have been grim humor as he approached her. His hairy breast, glistening with sweat and blood, heaved with his panting. Slowly and laboriously he reached up and cut her cords, then fell back against the wall and leaned there, his trembling legs braced wide. She scrambled up from where she had fallen and caught him in a frenzied embrace, sobbing hysterically.

"Oh, Conan, you are wounded unto death! Oh, what shall we do?"

"Well," he panted, "you can't fight a devil out of hell and come off with a whole skin!"

"Where is it?" she whispered. "Did you kill it?"

"I don't know. It fell into a pit. It was hanging in bloody shreds, but whether it can be killed by steel I know not."

"Oh, your poor back!" she wailed, wringing her hands.

"It lashed me with a tentacle," he grimaced, swearing as he moved. "It cut like wire and burned like poison. But it was its damnable squeezing that got my wind. It was worse than a python. If half my guts are not mashed out of place, I'm much mistaken."

"What shall we do?" she whimpered.

He glanced up. The trap was closed. No sound came from above.

"We can't go back through the secret door," he muttered. "That room is full of dead men, and doubtless warriors keep watch there. They must have thought my doom sealed when I plunged through the floor above, or else they dare not follow me into this tunnel.—Twist that radium gem off the wall.—As I groped my way back up the corridor I felt arches opening into other tunnels. We'll follow the first we come to. It may lead to another pit, or to the open air. We must chance it. We can't stay here and rot."

Natala obeyed, and holding the tiny point of light in his left hand and his bloody saber in his right, Conan started down the corridor. He went slowly, stiffly, only his animal vitality keeping him on his feet. There was a blank glare in his bloodshot eyes, and Natala saw him involuntarily lick his battered lips from time to time. She knew his suffering was ghastly, but with the stoicism of the wilds he made no complaint.

Presently the dim light shone on a black arch, and into this Conan turned. Natala cringed at what she might see, but the light revealed only a tunnel similar to that they had just left.

How far they went she had no idea, before they mounted a long stair and came upon a stone door, fastened with a golden bolt.

She hesitated, glancing at Conan. The barbarian was swaying on his feet, the light in his unsteady hand flinging fantastic shadows back and forth along the wall.

"Open the door, girl," he muttered thickly. "The men of Xuthal will be waiting for us, and I would not disappoint them. By Crom, the city has not seen such a sacrifice as I will make!"

She knew he was half delirious. No sound came from beyond the door. Taking the radium gem from his blood-stained hand, she threw the bolt and drew the panel inward. The inner side of a cloth-of-gold tapestry met her gaze and she drew it aside and peeked through, her heart in her mouth. She was looking into an empty chamber in the center of which a silvery fountain tinkled.

Conan's hand fell heavily on her naked shoulder.

"Stand aside, girl," he mumbled. "Now is the feasting of swords."

"There is no one in the chamber," she answered. "But there is water—"

"I hear it," he licked his blackened lips. "We will drink before we die."

He seemed blinded. She took his darkly stained hand and led him through the stone door. She went on tiptoe, expecting a rush of yellow figures through the arches at any instant.

"Drink while I keep watch," he muttered.

"No, I am not thirsty. Lie down beside the fountain and I will bathe your wounds."

"What of the swords of Xuthal?" He continually raked his arm across his eyes as if to clear his blurred sight.

"I hear no one. All is silent."

He sank down gropingly and plunged his face into the crystal jet, drinking as if he could not get enough. When he raised his head there was sanity in his bloodshot eyes and he stretched his massive limbs out on the marble floor as she requested, though he kept his saber in his hand, and his eyes continually roved toward the archways. She bathed his torn flesh and bandaged the deeper wounds with strips torn from a silk hanging. She shuddered at the appearance of his back; the flesh was discolored, mottled and spotted black and blue and a sickly yellow, where it was not raw. As she worked she sought frantically for a solution to their problem. If they stayed where they were, they would eventually be discovered. Whether the men of Xuthal were searching the palaces for them, or had returned to their dreams, she could not know.

As she finished her task, she froze. Under the hanging that partly concealed an alcove, she saw a hand's breadth of yellow flesh.

Saying nothing to Conan, she rose and crossed the chamber softly, grasping his poniard. Her heart pounded suffocatingly as she cautiously drew aside the hanging. On the dais lay a young yellow woman, naked and apparently lifeless. At her hand stood a jade jar nearly full of peculiar golden-colored liquid. Natala believed it to be the elixir described by Thalis, which lent vigor and vitality to the degenerate Xuthal. She leaned across the supine form and grasped the vessel, her poniard poised over the girl's bosom. The latter did not wake.

With the jar in her possession, Natala hesitated, realizing it would be the safer course to put the sleeping girl beyond the power of waking and raising an alarm. But she could not bring herself to plunge the Cimmerian poniard into that still bosom, and at last she drew back the hanging and returned to Conan, who lay where she had left him, seemingly only partly conscious.

She bent and placed the jar to his lips. He drank, mechanically at first, then with a suddenly roused interest. To her amazement he sat up and took the vessel from her hands. When he lifted his face, his eyes were clear and normal. Much of the drawn haggard look had gone from his features, and his voice was not the mumble of delirium.

"Crom! Where did you get this?"

She pointed. "From that alcove, where a yellow hussy is sleeping."

He thrust his muzzle again into the golden liquid.

"By Crom," he said with a deep sigh, "I feel new life and power rush like wildfire through my veins. Surely this is the very elixir of Life!"

"We had best go back into the corridor," Natala ventured nervously. "We shall be discovered if we stay here long. We can hide there until your wounds heal—"

"Not I," he grunted. "We are not rats, to hide in dark burrows. We leave this devil-city now, and let none seek to stop us."

"But your wounds!" she wailed.

"I do not feel them," he answered. "It may be a false strength this liquor has given me, but I swear I am aware of neither pain nor weakness."

With sudden purpose he crossed the chamber to a window she had not noticed. Over his shoulder she looked out. A cool breeze tossed her tousled locks. Above was the dark velvet sky, clustered with stars. Below them stretched a vague expanse of sand.

"Thalis said the city was one great palace," said Conan. "Evidently some of the chambers are built like towers on the wall. This one is. Chance has led us well."

"What do you mean?" she asked, glancing apprehensively over her shoulder.

"There is a crystal jar on that ivory table," he answered. "Fill it with water and tie a strip of that torn hanging about its neck for a handle while I rip up this tapestry."

She obeyed without question, and when she turned from her task she saw Conan rapidly tying together the long tough strips of silk to make a rope, one end of which he fastened to the leg of the massive ivory table.

"We'll take our chance with the desert," said he. "Thalis spoke of an oasis a day's march to the south, and grasslands beyond that. If we reach the oasis we can rest until my wounds heal. This wine is like sorcery. A little while ago I was little more than a dead man; now I am ready for anything. Here is enough silk left for you to make a garment of."

Natala had forgotten her nudity. The mere fact caused her no qualms, but her delicate skin would need protection from the desert sun. As she knotted the silk length about her supple body, Conan turned to the window and with a contemptuous wrench tore away the soft gold bars that guarded it. Then, looping the loose end of his silk rope about Natala's hips, and cautioning her to hold on with both hands, he lifted her through the window and lowered her the thirty-odd feet to the earth. She stepped out of the loop, and drawing it back up, he made fast the vessels of water and wine, and lowered them to her. He followed them, sliding down swiftly, hand over hand.

As he reached her side, Natala gave a sigh of relief. They stood alone at the foot of the great wall, the paling stars overhead and the naked desert about them. What perils yet confronted them she could not know, but her heart sang with joy because they were out of that ghostly, unreal city.

"They may find the rope," grunted Conan, slinging the precious jars across his shoulders, wincing at the contact with his mangled flesh. "They may even pursue us, but from what Thalis said, I doubt it. That way is south," a bronze muscular arm indicated their course; "so somewhere in that direction lies the oasis. Come!"

Taking her hand with a thoughtfulness unusual for him, Conan strode out across the sands, suiting his stride to the shorter legs of his companion. He did not glance back at the silent city, brooding dreamily and ghostily behind them.

"Conan," Natala ventured finally, "when you fought the monster, and later, as you came up the corridor, did you see anything of—of Thalis?"

He shook his head. "It was dark in the corridor; but it was empty."

She shuddered. "She tortured me—yet I pity her."

"It was a hot welcome we got in that accursed city," he snarled. Then his grim humor returned. "Well, they'll remember our visit long enough, I'll wager. There are brains and guts and blood to be cleaned off the marble tiles, and if their god still lives, he carries more wounds than I. We got off light, after all: we have wine and water and a good chance of reaching a habitable country, though I look as if I've gone through a meatgrinder, and you have a sore—"

"It's all your fault," she interrupted. "If you had not looked so long and admiringly at that Stygian cat—"

"Crom and his devils!" he swore. "When the oceans drown the world, women will take time for jealousy. Devil take their conceit! Did I tell the Stygian to fall in love with me? After all, she was only human!"

www.ingramcontent.com/pod-product-compliance
Lightning Source LLC
Chambersburg PA
CBHW020919180626
46816CB00007BA/2477